Almost a Meal

Almost a Meal
A True Tale of Horror

Stephanie C. Fox, J.D.

QueenBeeBooks

Bloomfield, Connecticut, U.S.A.

Library of Congress Cataloging-in-Publication Data
Name: Fox, Stephanie C., author.
Title: Almost a Meal – A True Tale of Horror / Stephanie C. Fox.
Description: Connecticut: QueenBeeEdit Books, [2012].
Identifiers: ISBN: 978-0-9996395-7-3 (paperback)
Subjects: 1. Horror—Fiction. 2. General—Fiction. 3. Psychological—Fiction.

www.queenbeeedit.com

Cover design by Stephanie C. Fox
Cover illustration by Bradford R. Conant
Printed in the United States of America

Also by Stephanie C. Fox

*Elephant's Kitchen
– An Aspergirl's Study in Difference*

An American Woman in Kuwait

*Scheherazade Cat:
The Story of a War Hero*

The Book of Thieves

*Nae-Née
Birth Control: Infallible, with
Nanites and Convenience for All*

*Vaccine: The Cull – Nae-Née Wasn't
Enough*

*New World Order Underwater:
The Nae-Née Inventors Strike Back*

What the Small Gray Visitor Said

*Hawai'i – Stolen Paradise:
A Travelogue*

*Hawai'i – Stolen Paradise:
A Brief History*

This story is dedicated to
Michelle Dorr.

*I became insane, with long
intervals of horrible sanity.*
-    Edgar Allan Poe

Almost a Meal
- A True Tale of Horror

It was his wife's opinion that it was the man's Asperger's that kept him from realizing that someone he knew decades ago, a chef who made him meals and played games of chess with him on Bluff Island, was a serial killer. That, and some luck.

The man definitely had Asperger's, which meant that he didn't emote even though he was capable of a full range of emotions. Different things might induce emotions in the man than the things that would work for a neurotypical, but despite the deadpan expression on his face, the man definitely felt things. He could feel great empathy for animals, particularly cats, sympathy for the downtrodden, and outrage over unfair or unequal treatment by society of those who are different. He could not, however, read very many expressions on other people's faces.

Perhaps that was why he felt such an affinity for his wife. She too had Asperger's, and she had studied it in enough depth to be able to articulate the condition. They had long talks about it, which were great fun and led to a greater understanding of their pasts.

That meant that many of these talks led to telling each other stories from the past.

Some of these stories were about things that had been long forgotten.

Almost a Meal

Life can cause people to forget things for years while they are busy doing and accomplishing and experiencing other things. Then, after years of thinking about these other things, something reminds them of what was once foremost in their thoughts and experience.

That was what led the man to tell his wife about this chef on Bluff Island.

The acquaintance was the result of the man's friendship with the chef's mother.

She often let the man stay in her son's room while he was away, and he was away often.

Almost a Meal

Neither the mother nor the man gave the chef's absences much thought.

Why should he? The chef had trained at the Culinary Institute of America in Hyde Park, New York, which was the top chef school in the United States. Although he had a room in his mother's house on Bluff Island, he could hardly be expected to spend the bulk of his time living there. It made sense that the chef was away a lot, presumably cooking great meals at restaurants on the mainland.

The man was occupied with his own problems and life, as people tend to be, and so he had plenty of things on his mind, and plenty to do. He also had many things that he felt he needed to accomplish. The man wanted to go back to school and earn his bachelor's degree. He wanted to return to active duty in the army. He wanted to earn a Ph.D. He wanted to travel some more. He never wanted to see his own family again.

Consequently, he did not notice or interpret what he saw or experienced of the chef.

The man knew that the chef and his mother did not get along. She called her son "Kristen" when she was drunk, and he hated that. There was real animosity between them, but it did not concern the man, nor did it affect his friendship with the mother.

She got along very well with everyone she knew, except for her son. As for the man, he got along with both of them. The chef was just four years older than the man, so they found things to talk about that interested them both.

When the chef was away, the man looked for a place to put his own things – clothes, hairbrush, razor, etc. – in the chef's bureau drawers. Busy with odd jobs on Bluff Island, the man didn't give much thought to what he found in them.

He found a large collection of women's and girl's clothing.

But, since he knew that the chef was a cross-dresser, the man hardly gave it a thought.

He shoved the lot of it out of the way after briefly puzzling over some odd characteristics of the chef's stash of female clothing: holes in the crotches of the panties, holes on the nipple-points of the bras held shut by safety pins and, oddest of all, clothing that was too small for an adult male cross-dresser to fit into. The extensive collection of women's jewelry commanded none of his attention. It followed that if the drawers were full of female clothing, then there would also be female jewelry in them.

But…the man was busy making his way on the island, and enjoying his friendship with a pretty little cat who lived in the house. He loved cats, and this one was always happy to see him. She would appear the moment that she heard his voice whenever he came back to the house. Whenever the man was distracted or anxious, he would think of that cat, and if he was in the house, he would go find her and pet her and talk to her.

When the chef was home on the island, the man stayed with other friends, or slept on the sofa in the house. During those visits, the chef liked to spend some of his spare time with the man. They would play chess together some evenings.

The man was a terrible chess player. He wanted to improve, but he just couldn't. Still, he kept trying, hoping that experience would teach him to play the game better.

The chef always beat him.

Perhaps it was just as well.

The chef seemed like a very nice guy. When they played chess, they would talk about interesting things – politics, history, war, travel, and the man's time in the army as a medic, which he had spent in Germany. But… now and then, when the topic of their conversations turned to the darker side of human nature, the man would observe a subtle change to occur in the chef's demeanor.

Upon hearing of some of the man's life experiences in which he was witness to death, strange sex, and other upsetting events, the chef would become very quiet and focused, projecting what seemed to be a mixture of longing and internal glee.

Almost a Meal

The man interpreted these reactions as evidence that the chef might be a kindred spirit – and was thus more than happy to continue drawing out and nurturing his friend's dark side. In later years, the man occasionally reflected that he should perhaps have been careful what he wished for, because although he would not be consumed by the darkness of the chef's soul, others would be.

As their friendship evolved, the man recognized that his interaction with the chef was fundamentally different from those that he had with others. The man's ability to use the native brilliance and creativity that are attributes of Asperger's for material gain within human society were blunted by his inability to read the plethora of social cues neurotypical people are finely attuned to.

This was not the case with the chef. The man found he could read the chefs expressions and interpret his body language with a high degree of precision…and that the converse was also true. In time, they came to value each other's friendship greatly.

But…the man sensed that the chef was fundamentally and spiritually different, and in a way that might include evil in some form. However, life as a person who was different from the majority had taught the man to despise the social compact after repeated bullying by members of that majority. Thanks to all that, without fearing for his own safety, the man watched the chef with increasing fascination.

Almost a Meal

The chef was surprisingly kind to animals, including an obnoxious, yapping little dog owned by his mother that even the man was tempted to stomp now and then. The man reasoned that the chef's affinity for animals meant that he posed no danger to humans. The man was wrong. He did not know until much later that the chef had tortured animals in the past. He did not realize that the chef, out of a sense of self-preservation, was concealing that predilection.

The man loved cats. If he had known about the chef's past with cats, his attitude would have been very different…but, no doubt, his continued ignorance and inability to see what was right in front of him was a large part of what kept him safe. The chef had decapitated the pets of his bullies when he was a child; the man had befriended a kitten as a child, and his bullies had broken every bone in her body and then left the tiny corpse in his bed at camp.

He did notice, however, that hidden elements of the chef's personality occasionally surfaced when the man had occasion to relate anecdotes from his past that tended to greatly disturb neurotypicals.

The man had a couple of stories that the chef thoroughly enjoyed hearing.

Years later, when he met his wife and told them to her, she enjoyed them too.

The stories were about unconventional and rather bizarre

things, things that could appear in a movie or a novel, so the fact that different people could like them was not odd. That amused the man, because the stories certainly were odd. Of course, as the old saying goes, truth is stranger than fiction. Both stories involved the name Harold.

One story was about the chief medical officer at a U.S. military hospital in Germany.

The doctor had a unique method of dealing with malingerers – soldiers who came to him to obtain notes excusing them from going out on training exercises.

The method had to do with the doctor's pet tarantula, whose name was Harold.

Almost a Meal

Harold lived in a glass terrarium with a heating lamp, and ate cockroaches.

The doctor had trained Harold to find his meals by following a trail of chicken soup. He would take a dropper, fill it with chicken soup, and drip some onto a cockroach. After Harold had learned to associate the scent of chicken soup with a meal, the doctor would dot the soup in a long line through the terrarium, and place a chicken-soup-scented cockroach at the end of it.

With that, he was ready to deal with the malingerers.

The doctor was a bald man, and his uniform included a shirt with a pocket on each side.

Almost a Meal

He put Harold in one pocket, a cockroach in the other, and dripped chicken soup in a trail that went from one pocket to the other…right over his own head.

When a malingerer showed up at the clinic, the doctor would unbutton his pockets.

Out would creep Harold the tarantula.

The doctor would completely ignore his furry arachnid pet as he continued the interview with the reluctant soldier, keeping his expression benign as he did so.

The man loved to watch; by the time that Harold was halfway up the side of the doctor's face, the malingerer would always be gone – out the door, ready for training exercises.

The chef thought that this was a great story – hilarious.

This was, of course, the expected reaction to the story.

The second Harold story was a bit more lurid, and the chef loved that one, too.

There was a necrophiliac at a medical school in Germany.

A necrophiliac is someone who loves dead bodies.

The necrophiliac had access to dead bodies, which made sense. What was the point of having a predilection for something that one couldn't get near, after all?

Almost a Meal

The man knew the necrophiliac, and he loved a good practical joke.

The man also was unconcerned about the fate of dead bodies – after all, they were dead, and their problems and feelings had ceased to be of concern to them, so he saw no reason for concern on his part.

The man's wife had some doubts about that attitude, but she wasn't overly concerned.

After all, she tended to pity the living more than the dead herself.

But back to the necrophiliac.

Very early one morning, the necrophiliac took a disembodied head that he had dubbed Harold up to the cafeteria, and put it into a juice machine.

The juice machine was one of those things that constantly churns a somewhat clear blend of juice in a large, raised tank, with nozzles below the tank and levers to push glasses against.

Harold the Head fit into it nicely.

The necrophiliac and the man moved out of sight and waited.

The first person to come into the cafeteria was an older, stocky, German woman.

She was a cleaning lady. She wore a cap over her hair, which was tucked under it, though a few loose strands stuck out. Her uniform was a plain, pale blue, with a striped apron. She had a bucket and a mop, and she was cleaning the floor.

The watchers stayed in their place of concealment, observing her progress as she worked her way across the floor and through the cafeteria. Steady motions, back and forth, then dunking the mop in her bucket, then back and forth again across each bit of linoleum. Before long, she had reached the juice machine.

As she worked, the cleaning lady glanced over her shoulder from time to time, perhaps to make sure that she wasn't bumping into anything.

She did so again as she paused in front of the juice machine, then stopped mopping.

With sudden, jerking, bobbing movements, she slowly looked up at the juice machine, resembling a robot as she did so.

Harold the Head chose that moment to roll around in the juice machine to face her, with a zombie-like, vacant stare as he turned in her direction.

What ensued next happened rather fast. Simultaneously, liquid brown trickled down the unfortunate woman's legs and vomit fired across the room as an abrupt, projectile stream. The mop hit the floor, and the cleaning lady fled with a shriek.

Harold the Head was retrieved and returned to his assigned storage place, but the juice machine was left otherwise undisturbed. The man did not drink that juice, of course.

That was it – the second Harold story.

That the name Harold wound up in both stories was just a coincidence.

Regardless, the chef found that one greatly amusing.

Sometimes, the chef would cook a delicious meal for the man, and they would chat as they ate it together. There might be one other guest to enjoy the food, or not. The meals were imaginatively prepared, pretty to look at on the plates, with lots of different flavors.

There was just one odd thing about them.

Almost a Meal

It was the meat.

What was it?

But the man was not the sort of person to give what he was eating much thought.

When his wife, who was a self-taught gourmet chef and baker, heard this detail, she laughed. She laughed because her husband was the last person she go to for a critical opinion about a new recipe. He would eat anything and like it. This made him wonderfully easy to please and appreciative of whatever she gave him, and that was great fun, but it wasn't conclusive proof of how good it actually was. She didn't care; she found other critics, who loved her food and praised it, and continued to spoil her husband with her skills.

So the fact that the man had eaten whatever was put in front of him by a C.I.A.-trained chef (what a wonderful acronym!) without questioning what any of it was had come as no surprise to her. That was par for the course – pun intended.

Once, the man had gone on a long hike over Bluff Island with a large group of people.

So had the chef.

Their party had included a young couple with a baby, who was being carried in a sling that fitted over the person carrying him, with his arms and legs sticking out. It was like a hiker's pack, with a similar feel and weight to it, but with human cargo.

Each person in the party took turns wearing the baby-pack, and when the man's turn had come, he had put it on with the baby on his back rather than on his front, facing away from him.

The chef was walking behind him.

At one point, the man glanced back and found that the chef was staring at the baby with an odd longing that looked like hunger.

The man had seen the chef look at him that way sometimes, but had dismissed it.

Now, however, he noticed it again, and the chef saw that.

Almost a Meal

The chef stopped staring at the baby.

But not for long; a little while later, the man heard an odd sound and looked around.

The chef was putting the baby's fingers in his mouth and seemed to be tasting them, savoring them, and feeling the shape of them with his tongue.

The man told him to stop.

It just wouldn't be good if the baby's parents saw that, he added.

The chef obliged.

The rest of the hike went by without any further incidents.

Almost a Meal

The man spent just one winter on Bluff Island before moving on, and lost touch with the chef. He went away to Rhode Island, attended college, and graduated with honors four years later, having completed a double major in biology and chemistry. It was his third attempt at college, and the third time had been the charm.

During the summer breaks of those years, he worked with a famous woman scientist at Brookhaven National Laboratory. She was like a mother to him, and encouraged him with his scientific career goals.

She also urged him to reconnect with his family. He did not want to do that; they had never accepted anything about the man's quirky and unconventional personality. His own mother, a woman who had been divorced or widowed so rapidly in succession by his father that it felt uncertain which had occurred first, had been smothering in her affections toward him. Not only that, but she had repeatedly taken him to psychiatrists as he acted out while growing up.

As a result, the man had received one misdiagnosis after another: mental retardation, schizophrenia, and so on. None of this surprised his wife, because Asperger's did not hit the psychiatry books of the English-speaking world until 1994; by then the man was 39 years old.

Almost a Meal

At his mother's instigation, the man had been given an I.Q. test when he was a child that he had deliberately messed up on, by answering incorrectly or with impossibly ludicrous answers. The test had said that he had the I.Q. of a mentally retarded person. But later on, he was tested again, and received a score of 168 – a genius. He wasn't playing with the test that time.

Nonetheless, his family was convinced that he would never do anything good or significant with his life. They steadily disapproved of him at every turn, even when he had gotten his pilot's license (for small, Cessna planes). Despite the fact that he had once taken one of his two younger sisters and the family cat up in the plane, done a zero-gravity loop that freaked out the cat and messed up the interior of the plane, that was the least of it.

After graduating from college, the man enrolled in an officer training program in the U.S. Army's chemical weapons program and was deployed to Kuwait for the war there. His mentor from Brookhaven at least succeeded in persuading him to contact his mother before going away. Against his better judgment, he did so, thinking that he would not survive the war.

When the man got back, the man spent a summer in the United States, and visited Bluff Island. He brought up the rear in a parade there, as the one veteran from the Kuwait War, following the older veterans of previous wars who lived on the island.

Almost a Meal

Soon he was back in Kuwait, doing research into the health effects of chemicals on the local population, retrieving a lovely little calico cat that he had met while a soldier at the end of the war. He and a Kuwaiti physician did some great work together, traded war stories, and developed a treatment that healed most of the patients they administered it to.

The man forgot all about the chef while he worked, which was natural because he was so busy. He was finally doing something that he had wanted to do since he had been a child, something that both of his parents had done, and both of his uncles. It was something that he had been repeatedly told that he would never be able to do: he was studying for his Ph.D.

Almost a Meal

While he did that, which was in central Connecticut, a process which took him several years but made him what his wife liked to call a human science encyclopedia, he met her in the library. They became best friends.

She met his cat and taught the man all she knew about cat care, including the healthiest foods to give the silky little black-and-orange-and-white calico feline.

She baked delicious cakes from scratch for his birthdays, and he didn't want to tell her that he didn't like his birthday, so he didn't. The cakes were just too much fun; she decorated one with chocolates that were shaped like anatomically correct human hearts and brains, and another with icing piped in the shapes of spiders, worms, and caterpillars. The man had a great time regaling the people in his graduate school laboratory with the tale of his army survival training in the woods of Germany: 2 weeks in the woods with 2 days' worth of supplies. He had lived on insects for twelve of those days.

No wonder he was such an appreciative eater of his wife's offerings.

While the man was applying to graduate school, he came across a news item that caught his attention: the chef had been arrested for murder. He was proven guilty and sentenced to 30 years in prison.

Almost a Meal

Midway through the man's immunology program, the chef was found guilty of a robbery and a second murder. He was given another 30-year sentence, plus a 10-year one for the robbery.

The police found his trophies – stolen jewelry from his victims – and the bodies.

The man found out about this in passing as he studied and researched and ran ELISA tray after ELISA tray through the lab, writing up hundreds of pages of results.

He stayed focused on his work, but…that odd expression that often crept over the chef's face on Bluff Island came back to mind whenever he thought of him. That expression of longing, hunger, and considering the situation with great care and calculation. The chef had looked at the man like that sometimes.

Now that reflected upon it, now that he knew all that he knew, he couldn't escape the thought that, several times – no, probably many, many times – he was…almost a meal.

About the Author

Stephanie C. Fox, J.D. is a historian, author, and editor. She is a graduate of William Smith College and the University of Connecticut School of Law.

She runs an editing service called *QueenBeeEdit*, which caters to politicians, scientists, and others, found at www.queenbeeedit.com.

Ms. Fox has written several books on a variety of topics, including the effects of human overpopulation on the environment, Asperger's, cats, and travel to Kuwait and Hawai'i.